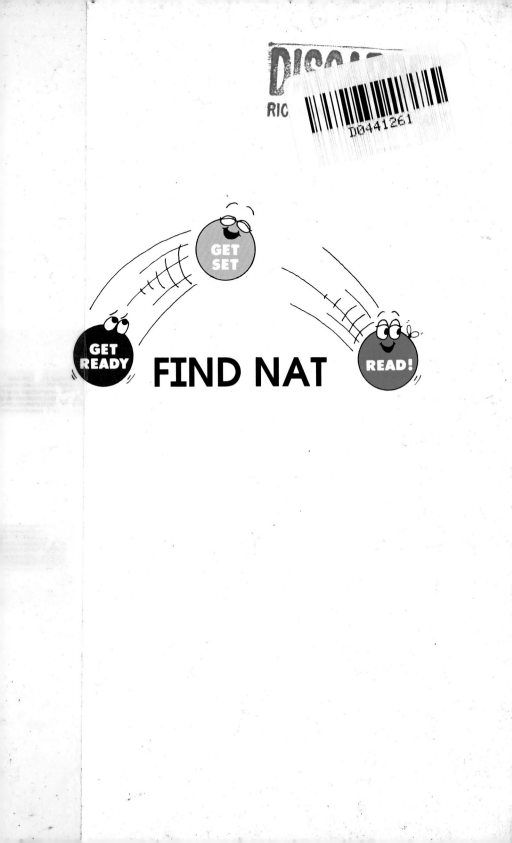

All inquiries should be addressed to:
Barron's Educational Series, Inc.
250 Wireless Boulevard
Hauppauge, New York 11788

ISBN-13: 978-0-8120-4678-6
ISBN-10: 0-8120-4678-1
Library of Congress Catalog Card Number 91-3113

Library of Congress Cataloging-in-Publication Data

Erickson, Gina Clegg.
    Find Nat / Gina Clegg Erickson and Kelli C. Foster :
illustrations by Kerri Gifford.
          p. cm.—(Get ready...get set...read!)
Summary: Through illustrations and rhyming text the reader
is invited to look for Nat the gnat among a group of animals.
        ISBN: 0-8120-4678-1
        (1. Animals—Fiction   2. Stories in rhyme.)
I. Foster, Kelli C.   II. Gifford, Kerri, ill.   III. Title.   IV. Series: Erickson,
Gina Clegg. Get ready...get set...read!
PZ8.3.E787Fi   1991
(E)—dc20   91-3113
                                                  CIP
                                                  AC

PRINTED IN CHINA

30 29 28 27 26 25

GET READY...GET SET...READ!

FIND NAT

by
Foster & Erickson

Illustrations by
Kerri Gifford

BARRON'S

Find Nat.
He is a gnat.

Is that Nat?

No.
That is a bat in a hat.

Is that Nat?

No.
That is a cat named Pat.

Is that Nat?

Yes.
That is Nat.

Splat!

Did the fat rat sit on Nat?

"No flat Nat,"
said the fat rat.

The bat in the hat,
the cat named Pat,
and the fat rat . . .

look for Nat!
Find Nat.

How about that?
You found Nat!

The End

The AT Word Family

Nat
bat
hat
cat
Pat
fat
rat
sat
flat
splat
that
gnat

Sight Words

a
for
how
the
you
find
look
said
about
found

Dear Parents and Educators:

Welcome to *Get Ready...Get Set...Read!*

We've created these books to introduce children to the magic of reading.

Each story in the series is built around one or two word families. For example, *A Mop for Pop* uses the OP word family. Letters and letter blends are added to OP to form words such as TOP, LOP, and STOP. As you can see, once children are able to read OP, it is a simple task for them to read the entire word family. In addition to word families, we have used a limited number of "sight words." These are words found to occur with high frequency in the books your child will soon be reading. Being able to identify sight words greatly increases reading skill.

You might find the steps outlined on the facing page useful in guiding your work with your beginning reader.

We had great fun creating these books, and great pleasure sharing them with our children. We hope *Get Ready...Get Set...Read!* helps make this first step in reading fun for you and your new reader.

Kelli C. Foster, PhD
Educational Psychologist

Gina Clegg Erickson, MA
Reading Specialist

Guidelines for Using *Get Ready...Get Set...Read!*

Step 1.   Read the story to your child.

Step 2.   Have your child read the Word Family list aloud several times.

Step 3.   Invent new words for the list. Print each new combination for your child to read. Remember, nonsense words can be used (*dat, kat, gat*).

Step 4.   Read the story *with* your child. He or she reads all of the Word Family words; you read the rest.

Step 5.   Have your child read the Sight Word list aloud several times.

Step 6.   Read the story *with* your child again. This time he or she reads the words from both lists; you read the rest.

Step 7.   Your child reads the entire book to you!

Titles in the

Series:

SET 1

Find Nat
The Sled Surprise
Sometimes I Wish
A Mop for Pop
The Bug Club
BRING-IT-ALL-TOGETHER BOOKS
What a Day for Flying!
Bat's Surprise

SET 2

The Tan Can
The Best Pets Yet
Pip and Kip
Frog Knows Best
Bub and Chub
BRING-IT-ALL-TOGETHER BOOKS
Where Is the Treasure?
What a Trip!

SET 3

Jake and the Snake
Jeepers Creepers
Two Fine Swine
What Rose Does Not Know
Pink and Blue
BRING-IT-ALL-TOGETHER BOOKS
The Pancake Day
Hide and Seek

SET 4

Whiptail of Blackshale Trail
Colleen and the Bean
Dwight and the Trilobite
The Old Man at the Moat
By the Light of the Moon
BRING-IT-ALL-TOGETHER BOOKS
Night Light
The Crossing

SET 5

Tall and Small
Bounder's Sound
How to Catch a Butterfly
Ludlow Grows Up
Matthew's Brew
BRING-IT-ALL-TOGETHER BOOKS
Snow in July
Let's Play Ball